Sometimes, when he was finding answers,
Archie made a little bit of mess ...

Why does toast make crumbs?

Why is milk splashy?

And sometimes Archie made a LOT of mess!

Time to clear up, Archie.

Oh, OK.

Why are there SO many bubbles?

Why do dropped things go SMASH?

Archie! Why don't you go and find Dad?

But wherever Archie went ...

...his questions went too.

Why is mud so sticky, Dad?

Why are these roots so long?

ARRGH!

Mum, **Why** do spiders have so many legs?

Archie's parents decided that a rhino with a LOT of questions might like a trip to the museum.

The museum was amazing.
There was SO much to see!

←Antiquities

Some of these questions were **easy** to answer...

PRESS HERE to hear me ROAR!

Tricera

Mum, **Why** aren't there any dinosaurs NOW?

...but others were a **little** more tricky.

Dad, **Why** does that man have such big ears?

Why is her nose so long?

Archie loved the museum. There were buttons – and knobs – and things which bleeped, buzzed and twanged!

Off he went –
here, there and
everywhere...

MANY wonderful whys later, there
was still SO much to find out.
   "Dad," said Archie,
now quite sleepy,
"why do ...

            robots ...

                    go ..."

YAWN!

Suddenly, all of Archie's questions stopped.

Archie was quiet **all** the way home.

And he didn't say a
word through teatime ...   OR bath time.

As they turned out his light, Mum and Dad wondered if Archie had run out of questions **completely.**

But why EVER would they think that?